KU-763-545

# Quackers

## The duck who didn't like to get his feet wet

Written by
**Denise Easson**

Illustrated by
**Joie Lamar**

BRAINSPIRED
PUBLISHING

Quackers by Denise Easson
Copyright © 2022 Denise Easson, All rights reserved.
1st Edition

Illustrations © 2022 by Joie Lamar, All rights reserved.

Cover design by Brainspired Publishing, JV., Creative team.

No part of this book may be reproduced in any form or by any electronic or mechanical means
including information storage and retrieval systems, without permission in writing from the author
publisher.
The only exception is by a reviewer, who may quote short excerpts in review.

This book is a work of fiction. The characters, their names, and actions are products of the author
imagination and are used fictitiously. Any resemblance to actual persons, living or dead is entire
coincidental.

ISBN: 978-1-7779490-5-1
Library and Archives Canada / Government of Canada

**BRAINSPIRED PUBLISHING**
A joint venture of Brainchild Holdings Inc. and INspired Media Inc.
Ontario, Canada.
www.brainspiredpublishing.com

# Hi

I hope you like duck stories because this one will quack you up.

**My name is** Quincifer – Usman – Aaron – Carlos – Kayden – Ethan – Rhys - Sam.

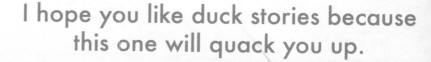

Momma calls me
QUACKERS
for short.

I think it's a great name for a duck.

I have 5 brothers and sisters and every morning, before the two-legged giants get up, Momma takes us on short walks to see how beautiful our world is

There are beautiful coloured flowers and trees and  grass that gives such a nice scent to the air.

We are still small, so can't walk too far, but I love these morning walks when everything is waking up and smelling fresh.

The only thing I don't really like is the wet dew on the ground  but it is nothing a young Duck can't handle.

One day Momma said it was time for a new adventure.  We walked along the soft grass and felt the warmth of the sunshine.  We stopped at a new place.

We waddled off the grass and onto something new called SAND that was soft on my feet.

Just beyond the SAND was something I had never seen before.

It was called a POND and was filled with something called WATER. When I took a closer look, my face was looking back at me.

I walked along the edge with my brothers and sisters and we saw all sorts of new sights in the water.

We saw small fish, frogs, turtles and plants.

Momma said this was an important day in our DUCK education. We were going to learn to swim!

We all got excited as we watched mom swim in the water. It looked like so much fun! She told us this was easy for baby Ducks and called us all in.

Everyone went in the big pond!

They were frolicking and quacking with joy at the fun they were having.

I dipped my webbed foot in, shook my head.   "Quack. Quack. Quack'.  I don't like to get my feet wet!

Momma said 'Whoever heard of a Duck that doesn't like to get their feet wet?  That's why we have 'webbed feet' made especially for swimming."

I just couldn't do it.  I didn't want to get my feet wet.

I sat out of the pond by a big shady tree and was softly crying.

A little two-legged giant came over and sat beside me and asked why I was so sad.

I told her I didn't like to get my feet wet.

She said she had never heard of a duck that didn't like the water.

She told me her name was Emily and we could be friends.

She told me not to cry and maybe we could think of a solution.

We thought and thought...

Then Emily said; 'I have a great idea! When it rains, I wear rubber boots that keep my feet dry and maybe you could get a pair!'

That night, when we were home in our nest, I told Momma about this idea.

She really wanted me to just go into the pond, but we agreed we could try this.

The next day she took me to the shoemaker.

He fixes shoes and he also makes special shoes for people.

Momma told him why we needed his help.

The shoemaker said; "I never heard of a Duck who doesn't like getting his feet wet! But I will try to make custom rubber boots just for him."

We returned to find the shoemaker had made me unique black boots with yellow Ducks on them.

They were made very wide so my feet would be comfortable.

I took to them like a 'Duck takes to water.'

That's a 'Duck Joke'.
Quack. Quack.
Quack.

When we got to the pond, I walked along the shoreline and watched the water cover the foot of my boots. My feet were dry. 'I LOVE my boots! I LOVE my boots!

Then Emily came by and said "Quackers! What beautiful rubber boots you have!"

My brothers and sisters were laughing and having fun playing in the water. They kept calling me to come in but I was happy to walk where the water meets the SAND.

They would say "Tomorrow's a new day, Quackers. Maybe you will be ready to join us!"

A few days later, after it had been raining, Emily and her friends passed by the pond on their way to school.

They were all wearing their rubber rain boots.

Emily told me she could jump in puddles and not get her feet wet.

I jumped into puddles with Emily and her friends.  It was so much fun.

Emily decided to walk into the pond.  Her friends told her this was not a good idea, but Emily didn't listen.  She kept walking.  She walked out to almost the middle of the pond!

Then something happened!

She had gone out too far!

The water started coming in over her boots and she was sinking!

Emily started crying out for help!

The boys and girls on the shore couldn't do anything because the water was too deep for them too.

I'm a Duck.  I knew I could safely swim, otherwise I would have 'QUACKED' for help.

Without thinking, I grabbed some rope that I found lying on the beach and ran into the water.

My boots started filling with water and then I started sinking!

Just then something happened!

My feet came out of the boots and because of my special webbed Duck feet, I was able to swim quickly to Emily.

Emily grabbed onto the rope. Me, Momma and my brothers and sisters were able to pull her to where she could stand up and walk out.

Emily was safe!

Her friends cheered!

Emily said "I will never
walk in a puddle that's
higher than my boot again

They all thanked us as they left.

Momma said "Quackers, I'm very proud of you. You didn't think of yourself. You saw that your friend needed help."

Momma and all my brothers and sisters said "We're proud of you Quackers!'

Oh, and by the way, I love playing in the water. It's so much fun!

My webbed feet are made especially for the water.

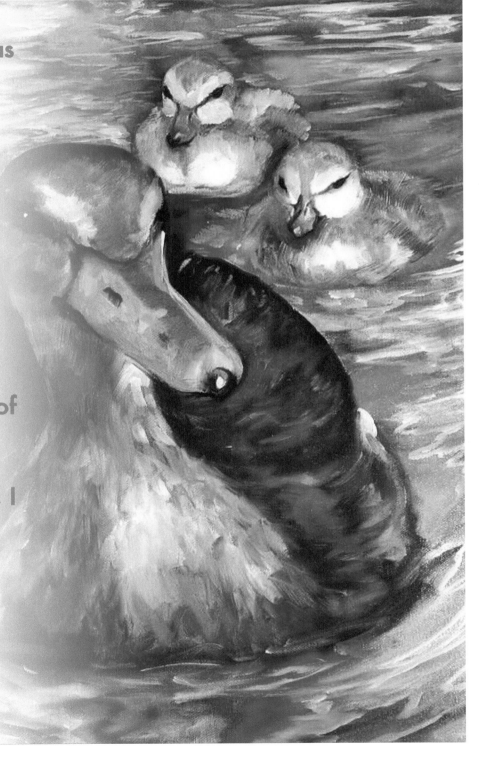

If you're walking by a pond and see Ducks, remember to wave.

It could be me!

# Quacker's Best Jokes

What has fangs and webbed feet?

Count Duckula

What do you call a Duck who is clever?

A wise quacker.

What do you call a Cow and two Ducks?

Milk and Quackers.

What TV shows to Ducks watch?

Duckumentries

You know why Ducks are good detectives?

They always Quack the case.

If a Duck says 'Quick. Quick' Wh does that mean?

He's got hiccups.

Which side of the Duck has more feathers?

The outside.

Knock. Knock. Who's there?
Quack.
Quack who?
Quack the door open and see.

The End

# About the Author

Denise Easson began her calling as a camp specialist and has developed an impressive curriculum vitae since then.

With a background in social work, her resume includes Director at a children's camp, engaging youth at risk in wilderness experiences, group homes, and working with mentally handicapped adults.

At present, she works in the adult addiction and mental health services sector, besides now being a children's book author. She keeps her love for life strong through 'glamping', kayaking, canoeing, hiking, equestrian activities, writing, and exploring new life experiences.

## About the Illustrations

Each illustration created by writer / artist *Joie Lamar* is a composition of acrylic paintings that she has exclusively created for this book, Quackers – The duck who didn't like to get his feet wet.

The paintings have been digitally collaged to create a unique visual experience for children and adults alike.

Printed in the USA
CPSIA information can be obtained
at www.ICGtesting.com
JSHW041712150224
57385JS00005B/15